Published by Fangamer, LLC **fangamer.com**

ISBN 978-0-9845032-4-7

First edition

We'd like to thank the following people for their feedback and support:

Shawne Benson, Ellen Zhou, Tyler Thompson, Jesse Hellman,

Debby Hellman, Ed Hellman, Gordon Salganik, Mitzi McClosky,

Elizabeth Kane Buzzelli, Patrice Thompson, C.B. Thompson,

Tessa Thompson, Vincenzo Barbetta, Devanshu Patel, Ryan O'Donnell,

Casey Muratori, Dale Beran, Paul Nestadt, Greg Rice, David Austin,

Byron Holz, Janani Sreenivasan, Katy Baggs, Brittany Aubert,

Laura Hudson, Talia Chriqui, Nolan Fabricius, Raber Umphenour,

Jeff Roberts, Amarisse Sullivan, Gary Hodges, Bret Victor, Nate Collins,

Derek Yu, Andrew Kelly, Stacy Cohen, Chris Furniss, Aaron Diaz,

Dorian Clair, Reid Young, Jon Kay, and Charlie Verdin.

This graphic novel was made possible by 1,594 Kickstarter backers in
November 2012. We are profoundly grateful for their support and wish to
express our deepest thanks. *Second Quest* simply would not
exist without them.

ART BY **DAVID HELLMAN**

 WRITTEN BY **TEVIS THOMPSON**

SECOND QUEST

for Shawne, who believed

for Ellen, who left

SECOND

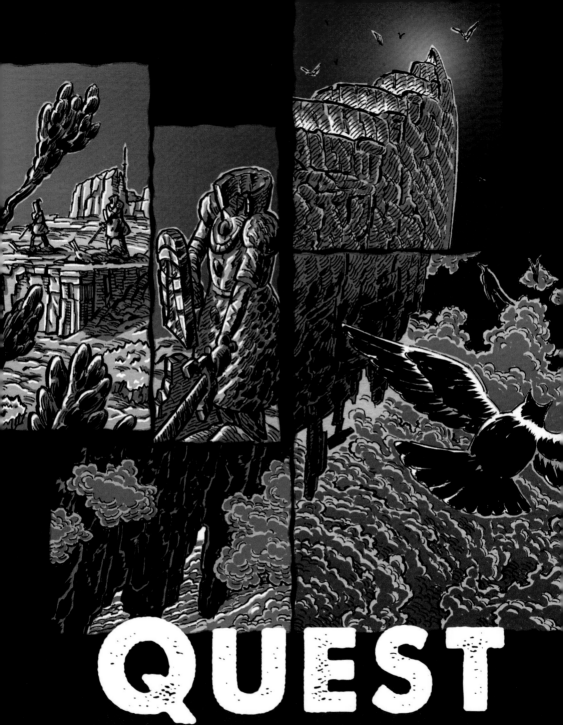

QUEST

Expedition 16:

The half-key I found is so beautiful.
But it's silent now, just like all my
other treasures. I know so many
hands have held it before mine.
For a moment today, I could almost
see them all. It's strange, an entire
world in such a small thing.

The last girl to
hold it disappeared
too quickly this time.
Why was she so frightened?
What was she like before?
I bet she dreamed of far-off
places too. I bet she searched
for hidden passages everywhere.
I bet she was just dying to tell
someone her secrets.

I can't help but wonder about every
girl I see. Could they look inside
things too? Was it enough? Or did
they feel this constant hunger?

Sometimes when I look at them,
I'm sure they're looking back at me.
I just feel, for a moment...seen.
But what is it they see?
Do they see who I really am?
Do they see what I'm looking for?
Do they see why I can't stop now?

Because there's still
no trace of you.

Something is happening. The visions have followed me here.
It's not just the relics anymore. It's like the world is
trying to show me something. And I want to see it.
I want to see.

I walk these streets and
everything looks different.
Things I've passed a
hundred times seem
strange and new.

I look through windows and there's
another woman, sitting alone in a room.
Have they always been this way? Did
I just never notice?

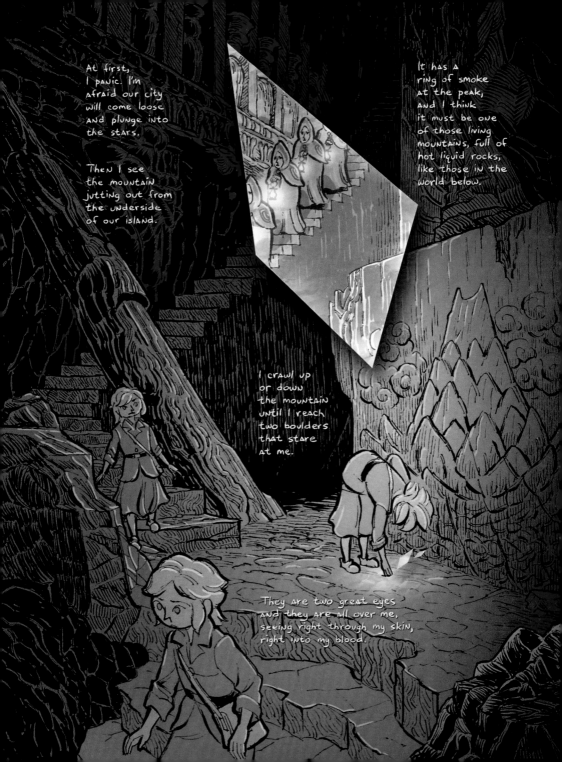

At first,
I panic. I'm
afraid our city
will come loose
and plunge into
the stars.

Then I see
the mountain
jutting out from
the underside
of our island.

It has a
ring of smoke
at the peak,
and I think
it must be one
of those living
mountains, full of
hot liquid rocks,
like those in the
world below.

I crawl up
or down
the mountain
until I reach
two boulders
that stare
at me.

They are two great eyes
and they are all over me,
seeing right through my skin,
right into my blood.

Between the
two rocks is a hole,
deep and dark and
full of voices.

The voices
whisper a name.

And it is my name.

AZALEA.

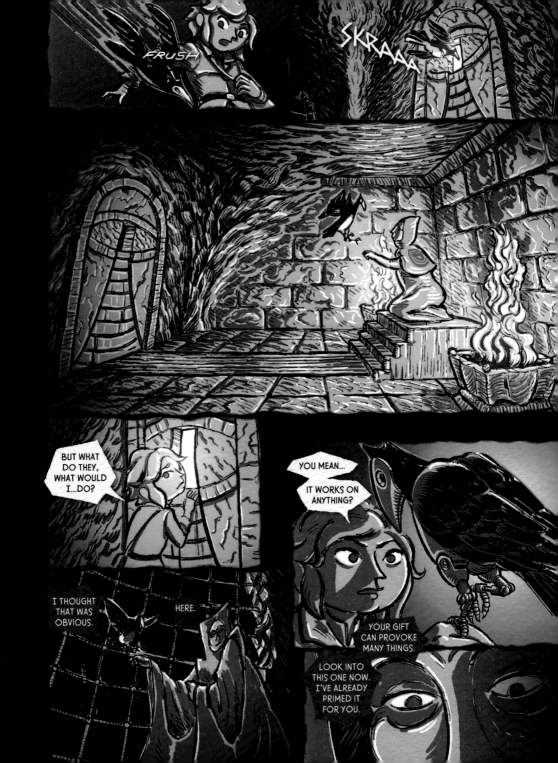

They say there's nothing left below.
But I don't believe them.

The world did not disappear just because we stopped looking.

I still dream
of places I have never been.

Of places I will never go.

I will remain here, Mother.
Where you left me.

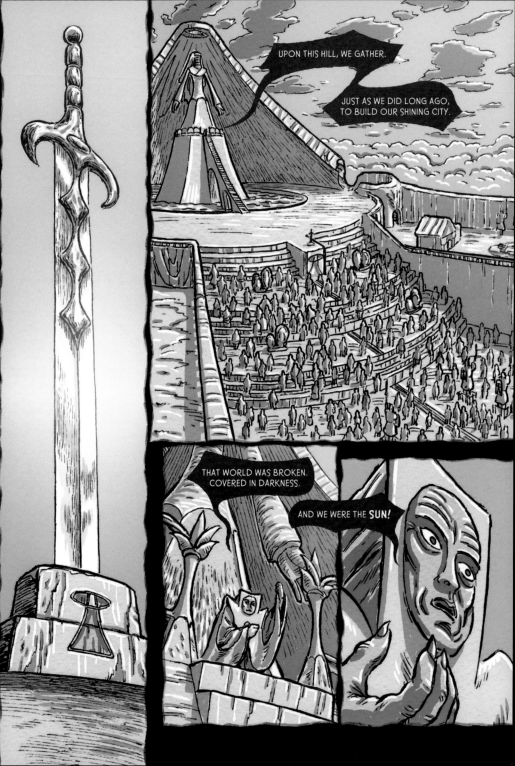

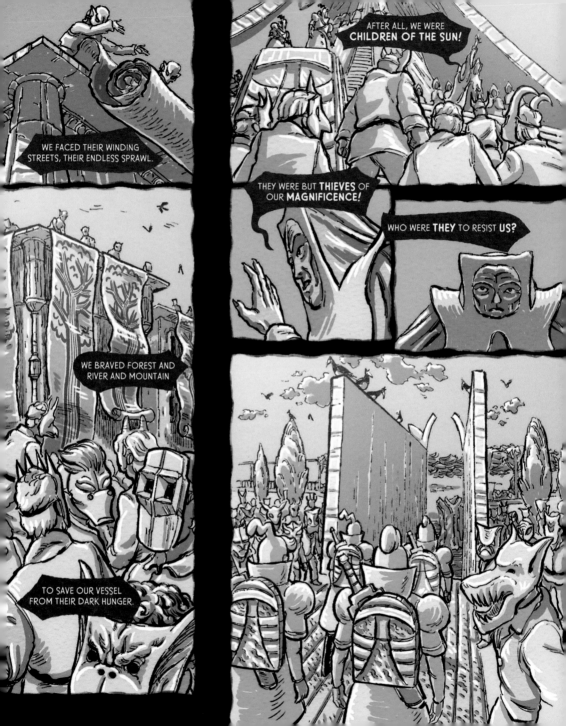

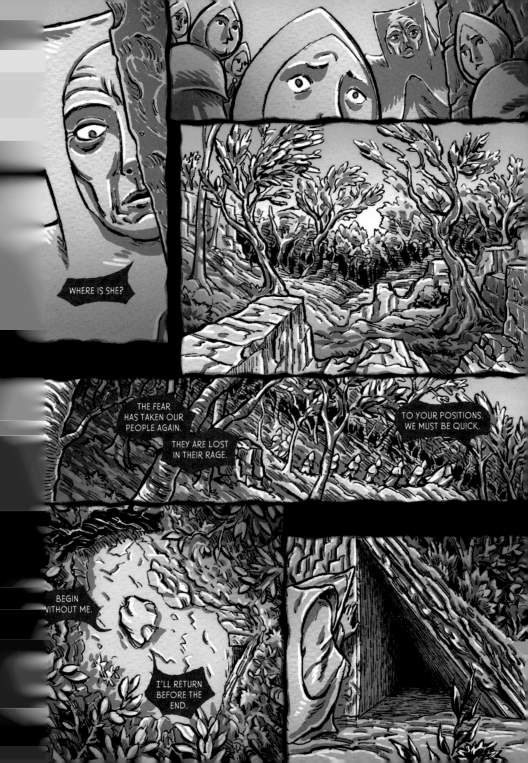

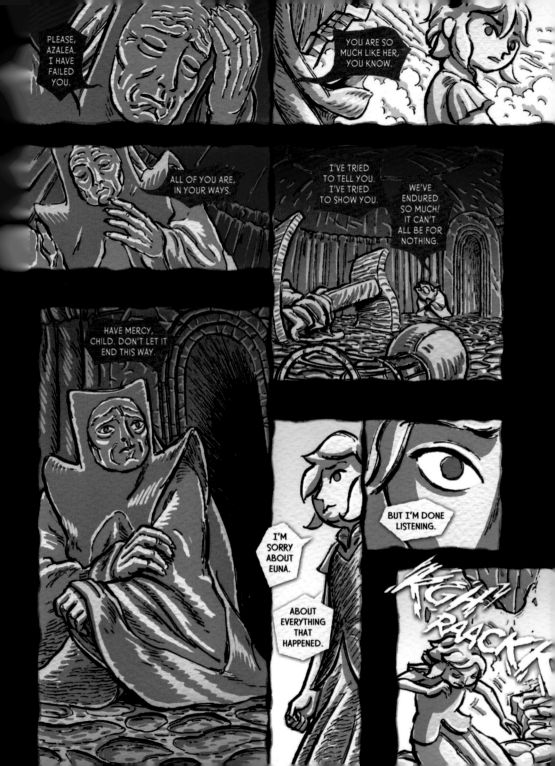

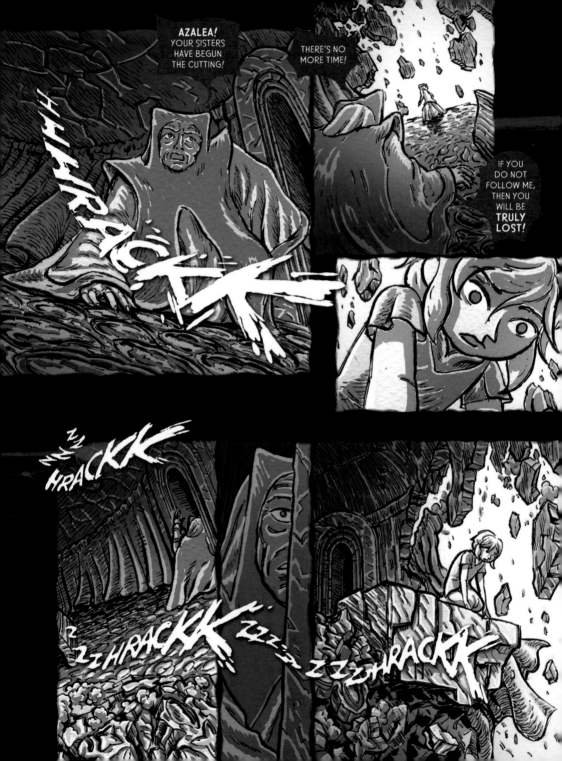

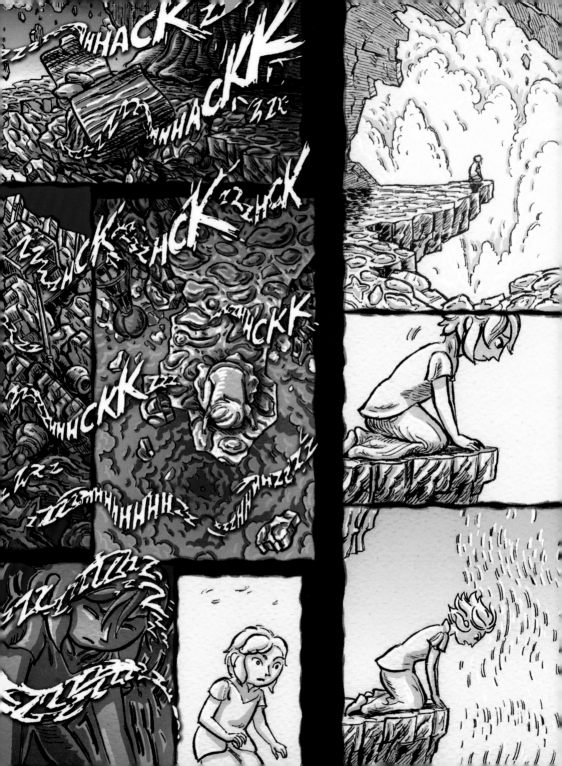

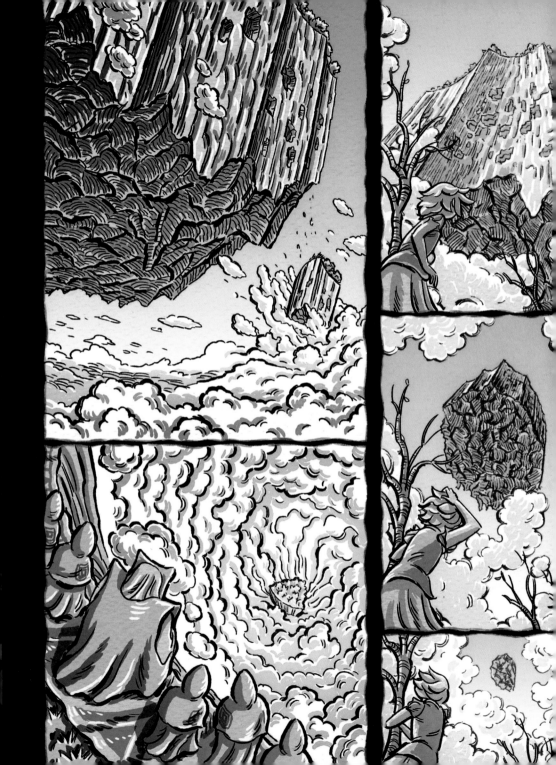

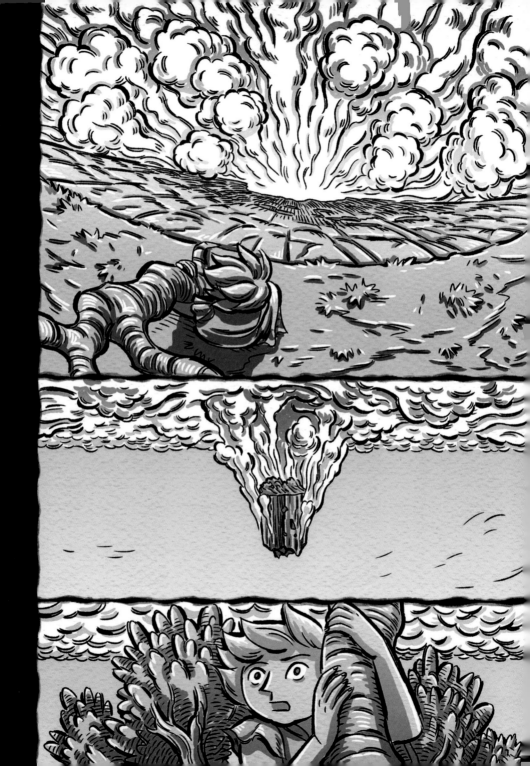